THE KING WHO SAVED HIMSELF

FROM BEING SAVED

BY JOHN CIARDI

DRAWINGS BY EDWARD GOREY

1965

J. B. LIPPINCOTT COMPANY   PHILADELPHIA   NEW YORK

BY JOHN CIARDI

You Know Who

John J. Plenty and Fiddler Dan

You Read to Me, I'll Read to You

The Man Who Sang the Sillies

Scrappy the Pup

The Reason for the Pelican

Jim Cubeta, Jimmy, James—
Hasn't he got a lot of names!
But James Cubeta, or Jimmy, or Jim—
All of us like all of him!
So here's an alakazam-kazimmy
For James Cubeta, or Jim, or Jimmy!
And here's an alakaziz-kazothers
For at least one—no, *both* his brothers!
And here's an alakazoz-kazummy
First for his Daddy and then for his Mummy!
Plus any three cheers you care to cheer
For whomever you care to write in . . . .
(here)

One Long Ago in a Far Away
Beginning "By the Sea"

In, of course, a Kingdom, One Fine Day
    With (why not?) a Lark in a tree.

(Yes, all the poems I ever see
    Put all their larks in the air.
Such poor tired larks! "Let one rest in my tree,"
    I thought. So I put it there.)

—So there *was* a Lark. In, as I say,
   The tree I put there to be
Part of that Long Ago Far Away
   Kingdom, of course, By the Sea.

A (naturally) Princess in (yes) a Tower
Was listening to (what else?) the Lark.

And a Ho-Hum Giant was smelling a flower
In the shade by the brook in the park.

The King was thinking of counting his gold
But went to sleep instead.

The Queen was hungry, but had a cold
 And hadn't got out of bed.

It was never as peaceful as this before
    In any fable I've read.
But in came a Hero. —At least he wore
    A helmet all over his head.

And he looked like a Hero (a very hard look).
    And he made a heroic noise.
And he clattered at every step he took
    (Which impressed the stable boys).

All *over* his head was his helmet and *in*
    His head was, of course, a fight.
And he came decked out in a suit of tin
    To prove that he was right.

He scared the Lark.

He woke the King.

The Princess began to cry.

The Queen got up and began to ring
For milk and an aspirin pie.

"Where is your Giant?" the Hero cried.
   "I have come to slay him in two!"
The Giant jumped up and ran off to hide
   In a closet. Wouldn't you?

"Where is your Giant?" the Hero roared.
  "I have come to do some slaying,
And save the Kingdom!" The King looked bored:
  "He's around here somewhere, playing."

"And now, if you please, be still," said the King.
    "We run a peaceful Kingdom.
If you must be heard, and if you can sing
    Some new songs, why then sing some.

"But stop that noise, young man, or I
    Shall toss you in that ocean
I always build my Kingdoms by.
    I don't like such commotion!"

But still the Hero stood his stand.
"Where is your Giant?" roared he.

"I have come to slay him and win the hand
    Of your daughter by setting you free!"

The Queen came in with a cold in her head
    And a cold in her nose, and her eyes
All sort of yellow and bleary red—
    Perhaps from the aspirin pies.

The Queen came in and she swayed a bit—
    Perhaps from the milk. "Tut! tut!"
She said to the Hero. "You're having a fit!
    You'll set us free? ——Of what?"

"I have come," said the Hero, "to set you free
    Of the Giant there always is
In every Kingdom By the Sea
    In such Long Ago days as this.

"And to win the hand of your daughter dear,
    And Half the Kingdom to boot!"

"*What?*" roared the King. "Get out of here,
Or I'll tell my guards to shoot!"

"I have come," said the Hero, "a very long way,
Over rivers, fields, and fences.

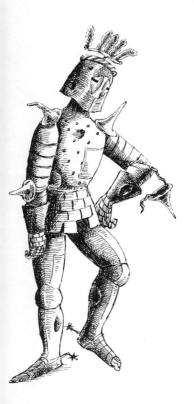

"I have been on the road six years and a day—
    Just think of my expenses.

"I've used twenty pounds of solder alone
    (Plus nuts and bolts and wire)
To mend my suit. And costs have grown
    Incalculably higher

"For sharpening swords, and for oats and hay.
   And heroes have to sip
A *little* something along the way
   ——To guard against the grippe.

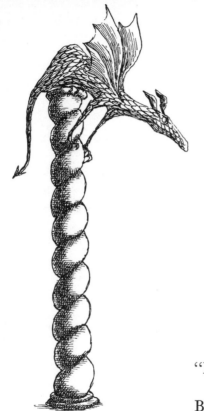

"I am not at all sure I can pay what I owe
  Out of half a Kingdom so small.
But Giants get scarcer and scarcer. So—
  It's this or nothing at all.

"And *enough* palaver! I'm here to do
   Some slaying, and here I stay
Till I have slain your Giant in two.
   So bring him on I say!"

"Well, then," said the King, "just wait a bit."
And he called his Cannoneer.

Who brought him a cannon and pointed it
    In a way that made it clear

The palaver *was* over. "That's unfair!"
    Cried the Hero.

"So it is,"
Said the King with a sigh. "You have me there.
But in Long Ago Kingdoms like this

"We have to be careful. It takes time
To become a Long Ago.
And though being a Hero is hardly a crime,
We do better without them, you know.

"A peaceful Kingdom's the Kingdom for me,"
        Said the King. "And as for you,
Go save someone else. For—do you see?—
        I dislike being saved in two.

"Heroes are handsome and noisy and bold
    But they *will* come out on top.
And once they start saving you, I've been told,
    They don't know when to stop.

"I run a peaceful Kingdom here
    And I'd like it to age **a** bit.

"—To which, may I add that my Cannoneer
Informs me his fuse is lit?

"You have *ten* seconds. I mean, *nine*."
    "Unfair!" the Hero cried.
"*Eight*," said the King. "You do look fine
    But—*seven*—a fast ride

"Could—*six*—prevent some changes you
    Might—*five*—not wish for—*four*—
(Or is it *three?*) Well, now it's *two* . . .
    One . . . and—What *is* that roar!

"A cannon? Why on earth?—Oh, yes,
    Now I remember. Well,
I tried to tell him. But I guess
    Heroes are hard to tell.

"Someone go let the Giant out

"And ask the Lark to sing.

"And, I say, isn't it about
   Dinner time?" said the King.

. . . And that's how it went One Long Ago
      And Far Away by the Sea,
Just as a Little Bird I know
      (A Lark) told it to me.

The Kingdom was saved from being saved.
The Giant was saved from a fight.

The King *was* afraid he had behaved
    In ways not entirely right.

"But *there* was the fuse, and it was lit,"
    He said, "and time ran on.
And before I had finished explaining it
    To the Hero, he was gone.

"In—I'm afraid—a sudden puff
    That puffed him out of sight.
As Heroes go, he was brave enough,
    But I'm not sure he was bright.

"I'm sure I made it perfectly clear
    What sort of Kingdom I run.
Why I even scolded my Cannoneer
    For firing that horrible gun.

"And I'm sure—had *I* stood where the Hero stood,
    All mounted and ready to go—
I'm sure I could have understood
    In, say, two seconds or so

"That only eight were left to me.
    And I'm sure that, given the eight,
I could have made it easily.
    Out of the palace gate.

"—Well, maybe not. But if it's true
     That, maybe, I misbehaved,
At least I wasn't saved in two.
     In fact, I wasn't saved.

"Except from *being saved*," he said.
     Which is all the saving *I'm* for."

. . . And that's that, friends. And so to bed.
For that is all there's time for.